SPIDER-MAN®
UNMASKED

SPIDER-MAN
UNMASKED

Entries Written By

MARK BERNARDO
PETER SANDERSON
BOB BUDIANSKY

Featuring the Artwork of

Pencilers

SAL BUSCEMA
SHAWN MCMANUS
MIKE WIERINGO
RON FRENZ
DAN JURGENS
JOHN ROMITA JR
RON GARNEY
MARK BAGLEY
DARICK ROBERTSON
PAT OLLIFFE
JOHN ROMITA SR

JOE BENNETT
PARIS KAROUNOS
GREG LUZNIAK
MARK BUCKINGHAM
ANDREW WILDMAN
TODD MCFARLANE
BILL REINHOLD
MIKE ZECK
TOM MORGAN
JACK KIRBY

Inkers

JOHN STANISCI
BILL SIENKIEWICZ
SAL BUSCEMA
RICHARD CASE
JOHN ROMITA SR
KLAUS JANSON
AL WILLIAMSON
LARRY MAHLSTEDT
RANDY EMBERLIN
JEFF ALBRECHT
AL VEY

AL MILGROM
JIMMY PALMIOTTI
MARK BUCKINGHAM
STEPHEN BASKERVILLE
MARK MCKENNA
JOE RUBENSTEIN
TODD MCFARLANE
BILL REINHOLD
BOB MCLEOD
JACK KIRBY

Editors
**TOM BREVOORT
and
ERIC FEIN**

Editor in Chief
BOB HARRAS

Cover by
**SCOTT MCDANIEL
and
KLAUS JANSON**

Cover Colorist and Separator
KEVIN TINSLEY

Book Design by
**COMICRAFT'S
JOHN MARASIGAN**

MARVEL
COMICS
M

SPIDER-MAN® UNMASKED Published by MARVEL COMICS. David J. Schreff, President. Stan Lee, Publisher. Shirrel Rhoades, Executive VP, Publishing. OFFICE OF PUBLICATION: 387 PARK AVENUE SOUTH, NEW YORK, N.Y. 10016. Copyright © 1996 Marvel Characters, Inc. All rights reserved. Price $5.95 per copy in the U.S. and $8.35 in Canada. GST #R127032852. No similarity between any of the names, characters, persons, and/or institutions in this magazine with those of any living or dead person or institution is intended, and any such similarity which may exist is purely coincidental. This periodical may not be sold except by authorized dealers and is sold subject to the condition that it shall not be sold or distributed with any part of its cover or markings removed, nor in a mutilated condition. SPIDER-MAN (including all prominent characters featured in this issue and the distinctive likenesses thereof) is a trademark of MARVEL CHARACTERS, INC. Printed in the U.S.A. First Printing, November, 1996. ISBN 0-7851-0275-2.

10 9 8 7 6 5 4 3 2 1

SOMETIMES THE MOST EXTRAORDINARY THINGS HAVE THE MOST ORDINARY BEGINNINGS. FOR EXAMPLE:

PETER PARKER WAS A NORMAL HIGH SCHOOL STUDENT, LOVED DEARLY BY THE UNCLE AND AUNT WHO RAISED HIM.

BUT WHILE HE EXCELLED AT SCIENCE, THOSE ACCOMPLISHMENTS WERE OFTEN OVER-SHADOWED BY HIS INNATE SHYNESS.

ER, WOULD ANYONE LIKE TO GO TO THE NEW EXHIBIT AT THE SCIENCE HALL WITH ME?

GET LOST, BOOKWORM!

IT WAS, HOWEVER, THAT SAME DEVOTION TO SCIENCE THAT WAS TO BRING ABOUT A MONUMENTAL CHANGE IN THE BOY'S LIFE!

FOR ONE DAY, AT AN ATOMIC ENERGY DEMONSTRATION, A TINY SPIDER ABSORBED A FANTASTIC AMOUNT OF RADIATION--

--AND IN SUDDEN SHOCK, BIT THE NEAREST LIVING THING!

OW!

WH-WHAT'S HAPPENING? I FEEL STRANGE!

AS IF MY ENTIRE BODY WERE CHARGED WITH SOME SORT OF WEIRD ENERGY!

BEEEP

OH, MY GOSH! I-I LEAPED HALFWAY UP THIS BUILDING!

A-AND I'M ACTUALLY CLINGING TO THE WALL JUST BY TOUCHING IT!

INCREDIBLE! I WALL-CRAWLED TO THE ROOF IN SECONDS! A-AND I'M CRUSHING THIS STEEL PIPE LIKE IT WAS *PAPER!*

IT'S AS IF I'VE SUDDENLY GAINED THE ABILITIES AND PROPORTIONAL STRENGTH OF... OF A *SPIDER!*

USING HIS TECHNICAL INGENUITY, YOUNG PARKER DEVELOPED DEVICES TO "SPIN" HIS OWN STICKY WEBBING!

AND THEN, AFTER DESIGNING A SUITABLY THEATRICAL COSTUME--

--HE SET OUT TO TAKE SHOW BUSINESS BY STORM--

--AS THE SPIDER-MAN!

BUT HIS EGO SWELLED WITH HIS FIRST TASTE OF FAME AND SUCCESS.

HE ALLOWED A THIEF TO ESCAPE, WHEN IT WOULD HAVE BEEN SO EASY TO STOP HIM, FIGURING IT WASN'T *HIS* PROBLEM!

HE DISCOVERED HOW *WRONG* HE WAS DAYS LATER, WHEN HE RETURNED HOME TO FIND POLICE THERE. THE HOUSE HAD BEEN BURGLARIZED--

--AND HIS BELOVED UNCLE BEN HAD BEEN SHOT *DEAD!*

WITH TEARS OF RAGE AND LOSS STINGING HIS EYES, HE SWORE HE'D BRING THE MURDERER TO JUSTICE!

BUT WHEN HE CAUGHT THE CULPRIT, HE WAS STUNNED TO FIND IT WAS THE SAME THIEF HE HAD LET ESCAPE BEFORE!

IT WAS A BITTER LESSON, ONE THAT CHANGED HIM EVEN MORE DEEPLY THAN THE BITE OF A RADIO-ACTIVE SPIDER!

FOR AT LAST HE GRASPED THE BASIC TRUTH THAT HAS SHAPED HIS LIFE EVER SINCE: WITH GREAT POWER, THERE MUST ALSO COME GREAT RESPONSIBILITY!

AND IT IS THIS, ABOVE ALL ELSE, THAT HAS GIVEN THE WORLD THE ONE, THE ONLY... THE AMAZING...

SPIDER-MAN!

DAVID MICHELINIE — WRITER
SAL BUSCEMA — ARTIST
CHRIS ELIOPOULOS (NEEDS SHORTER NAME) — COLORIST
EVAN SKOLNICK — COLORIST
DANNY FINGEROTH — EDITOR
TOM DEFALCO — ED IN CHIEF

BASED ON THE ORIGINAL STORY BY STAN LEE & STEVE DITKO

The BITE of a RADIOACTIVE SPIDER years ago endowed PETER PARKER with the INCREDIBLE POWERS that made him the AMAZING SPIDER-MAN.

OW!

"Really? That leads to some very interesting speculation!"

"MAYBE, BUT NOW IS NOT THE TIME TO GO INTO IT!"

His HANDS and FEET can CLING to sheer WALLS and even to CEILINGS as if they had THOUSANDS of tiny SUCTION CUPS attached!

What you notice FIRST on seeing SPIDER-MAN is the way he MOVES differently than ANYONE else!

In actuality, SCIENTISTS claim that SPIDER-MAN can somehow INCREASE the ATTRACTION between the MOLECULES of his BODY and those of the SURFACES he climbs!

This ability FOCUSES through his HANDS and FEET. It even WORKS if his hands and feet are COVERED by CLOTH, like his COSTUME.

However, if SPIDEY finds himself FORCED to SCALE a WALL as PETER PARKER, he always REMOVES his SHOES first. Apparently the molecular attraction CANNOT travel through a thick substance like SHOE LEATHER!

Spidey's OTHER famous means of TRAVEL is by SWINGING from the ROOFTOPS with his WEBBING. Spinning webs is NOT actually one of Spidey's SUPER-POWERS.

As PETER PARKER, he invented his WEB FLUID, which he FIRES from the WEB-SHOOTERS worn on his WRISTS.

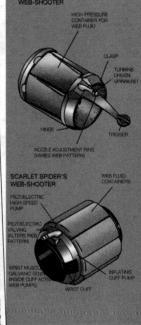

SPIDER-MAN'S WEB-SHOOTER

HIGH-PRESSURE CONTAINER FOR WEB FLUID

CLASP

TURBINE-DRIVEN SPINNERET

HINGE

TRIGGER

NOZZLE ADJUSTMENT RING (VARIES WEB PATTERN)

SCARLET SPIDER'S WEB-SHOOTER

WEB FLUID CONTAINERS

PIEZOELECTRIC HIGH-SPEED PUMP

PIEZOELECTRIC VALVING (ALTERS WEB PATTERN)

INFLATING CUFF PUMP

WRIST MUSCLE (GALVANIC SENSE INSIDE CUFF ACTIVATES WEB PUMPS)

WRIST CUFF

This artificial WEBBING has ENORMOUS strength, yet it DISSOLVES into POWDER in about TWO HOURS.

Moreover, Spidey can FORM the WEBBING into ANY SHAPE he can IMAGINE, like NETS, HAMMOCKS, or even PARACHUTES!

LONG HOURS OF PRACTICE TO THE OPERATION OF HIS WEB, THE TERRIFIC TEEN-AGER CAN NOW USE IT IN MANY DIFFERENT WAYS...

As a SHIELD...

A PARACHUTE...

A SAFETY NET...

As SKIIS...

As a RAFT...

As a CLUB...

OR PLAIN, SIMPLE STICKY GLUE!

A BARRIER...

A BALL

Just as a SPIDER or an ANT can carry MANY times its own WEIGHT, so too SPIDER-MAN is MANY times STRONGER than a NORMAL human being.

Spider-man can lift up to 10 tons above his head, making him a full 25 times stronger than a normal man.

("WHILE MY SUPER STRENGTH DOESN'T APPROACH THE POWER OF SOME OF THE HEAVIER HITTERS AROUND")

("...THE COMBINATION OF ALL MY SPIDER ABILITIES PUTS ME ON A PAR WITH ALMOST ANYONE!")

ENOUGH!!

Nevertheless, even SPIDER-MAN is far OUTMATCHED by many of his ALLIES and ENEMIES. THOR and the HULK can each lift over 100 TONS!

But Spidey's sheer DETERMINATION to WIN helps him HOLD his own against STRONGER foes.

WHOA!

(ONCE MY REFLEXES CAN OPERATE AS MUCH AS FORTY TIMES FASTER THAN A NORMAL PERSON'S, I OFTEN USE THEM TO PUZZLE A MUCH STRONGER...)

Once he even succeeded in KNOCKING OUT the HULK!

Spider-Man's REFLEXES are FIFTEEN times FASTER than a NORMAL man's! On top of that, his AGILITY is SUPERHUMAN. He can even DODGE BULLETS if he is far enough away!

With a single LEAP, Spider-Man can COVER the WIDTH of a city STREET, or rise THREE STORIES into the AIR!

SOMETHING ABOUT THAT MAN IS BOTHERING ME, BUT... WHAT IS IT?!

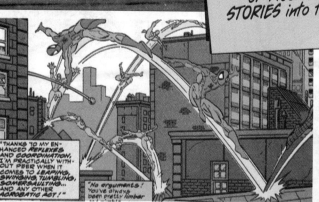

("THANKS TO MY EN-HANCED REFLEXES AND COORDINATION, I'M PRACTICALLY WITH-OUT PEER WHEN IT COMES TO LEAPING, SWINGING, TUMBLING, SOMERSAULTING... AND ANY OTHER ACROBATIC ACT!")

"No arguments! You've always been pretty limber."

The STRANGEST of all Spider-Man's POWERS is his SPIDER-SENSE. This is a form of EXTRA-SENSORY PERCEPTION that ALERTS him to DANGER by a TINGLING feeling in the BACK of his HEAD.

Spider-Man's SPIDER-SENSE enables him to FIND his ADVERSARIES even if he CAN'T see them.

Spider-Man can also TRACK DOWN people through his own INVENTION, the SPIDER-TRACER.

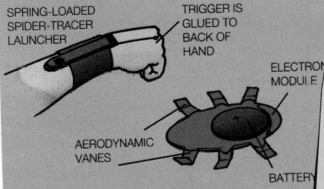

SPRING-LOADED SPIDER-TRACER LAUNCHER

TRIGGER IS GLUED TO BACK OF HAND

ELECTRONIC MODULE

AERODYNAMIC VANES

BATTERY

All he need do is to ATTACH the TRACER to the PERSON he needs to TRAIL.

His SPIDER-SENSE then picks up the Tracer's HOMING SIGNALS, so he can TRACK them down.

It's further PROOF that Spider-Man's GREATEST asset is NOT his SUPER-POWERS but the BRILLIANT MIND that CAME UP with his amazing INVENTIONS!

PETER PARKER

The son of secret agents Richard and Mary Parker, young Peter was orphaned at an early age, when his parents were declared missing in action during an undercover operation for the peace-keeping organization known as S.H.I.E.L.D. The boy was taken in by Richard's brother, Ben, and his wife May, and raised as their own child.

Peter quickly demonstrated an aptitude for the sciences, winning awards for his science fair project about the adhesive properties of certain molecule chains. His Aunt May and Uncle Ben encouraged him in his studies, scraping to save enough to buy Peter a microscope, even though money was tight. Peter hoped to one day become a great scientist like Reed Richards or Henry Pym.

But Peter's successes in the laboratory belied his problems socially. A shy child, Peter was constantly harassed and ridiculed by his fellow students due to his bookish demeanor. High school quarterback Flash Thompson in particular seemed to relish any opportunity to stick it to "Puny Parker".

Peter was a lonely, ostracized young man without a friend in the world, and with a growing resentment towards his peers building up inside him. And so he might have remained, had fate in the form of a radioactive spider not taken a hand...

MAY PARKER

The closest person in Peter Parker's life, May Reilly Parker has been a mother, a friend, a confidant, a voice of reason, a dispenser of advice, a sympathetic ear, and a guiding influence to the young man who would become the amazing Spider-Man. She and her husband, Ben Parker, adopted young Peter after the tragic deaths of his parents, and did their best to instill a sense of fairness, honesty and responsibility in the boy. When Ben was killed by a burglar soon after Peter started his career as Spider-Man, May carried on raising Peter herself. She didn't realize until much later the crushing burden of guilt her nephew carried with him because of his failure to prevent his uncle's death, and because of the constant lying to her that his double life as Spider-Man necessitated. For various reasons, Peter never was able to tell his loving aunt that he was Spider-Man. He felt the shock would be too much for her weak heart, or that she would be horrified that Peter was also the mysterious masked crimefighter that she so despised.

Always a sickly woman, May recently succumbed to a massive stroke that proved to be fatal. Before she passed away, however, she let Peter know that she had figured out that Peter was Spider-Man, and that her subconscious, constant refusal to believe it was what led to her hatred of the wall-crawler. Before breathing her last, May Parker told Peter she understood why he had done what he did, and gave her blessing on his life as Spider-Man.

FRIENDS OF SPIDER-MAN

The spirit of Ben Parker is, in the truest sense of the word, the reason why Spider-Man exists. When Peter's parents died unexpectedly when he was very young, Ben and his wife May took in the boy and raised him as their own. Ben raised Peter as the son he and May never had, and Peter certainly loved and admired his Uncle Ben as if he were his natural father. Despite his problems fitting in with his peers at high school, Peter always had the refuge of his surrogate family to escape to.

Tragedy struck Peter's life soon after the accident that gave him his amazing spider-powers. As Spider-Man, Peter intended to use his abilities for nothing more than his own fame and fortune, until a burglar whom Spider-Man let get away back at the TV studio broke into the Parkers' home and killed Uncle Ben. The vengeful young Spider-Man captured the burglar, and after seeing the face of the man who took the life of his beloved Uncle, learned the hardest lesson of his life: that with great power, there must also come great responsibility. In that moment of revelation, Spider-Man was truly born — not a costumed glory-seeker, but a true hero of whom his Uncle Ben could be proud.

BEN PARKER

MARY JANE WATSON-PARKER

For years, Spider-Man avoided meeting the mysterious niece of Aunt May's friend, Anna Watson. Anyone his aunt was trying to fix him up with, he reasoned, had to be a dud! His trepidation disappeared when he saw the vivacious red-haired party girl she truly was. This is the woman who was destined to become Peter Parker's wife.

From casual acquaintances to friends to lovers to husband and wife, Peter and Mary Jane's relationship has been a rocky road indeed. It was only in recent years that Peter discovered that part of the reason for her initial casual attitude toward their relationship was that she had long known that he was also Spider-Man, and feared getting close to him because of the dangers involved in his double life. However, their feelings for each other proved powerful enough to overcome all doubts and fears, and they were wed soon afterward.

Their married life has proven no less turbulent, as Mary Jane has tried to adjust to her husband's peril-fraught career as a costumed crimefighter. They have been dealt perhaps their strongest emotional blows of all in recent months, as Peter descended fully into his Spider-Man identity after the "deaths" of the beings claiming to be his parents. A pall was cast upon their happiness once again when a far-reaching revenge scheme convinced Peter that he was merely a clone of the original Peter Parker, and he was again driven to the edge of despair. Peter and Mary Jane's love has sustained them even through this crisis, and Peter has since been revealed to indeed be the original Spider-Man.

FRIENDS OF SPIDER-MAN

A longtime friend of Peter Parker's Aunt May, Anna Watson played a significant role in Peter's life by introducing him to her niece — his future wife, Mary Jane Watson! When Anna and May attempted to play matchmaker for their niece and nephew, Peter avoiding the arranged meeting for years, afraid of finding Mary Jane unattractive or incompatible. Mary Jane had her own issues that had her avoiding the meeting as well — such as the fact that she had discovered Peter was Spider-Man! But when the two young people finally met face-to-face, Peter was pleasantly surprised — and MJ found herself attracted to Peter despite his dark, dangerous secret. Years later, after much trial and tribulation, May and Anna's matchmaking paid off, as the two were wed.

Anna has become much closer to the Parker family since the marriage, even moving back to New York from her retirement home in Florida. She has helped Mary Jane through a personal crisis when Peter was losing himself in his Spider-Man persona and neglecting his marriage and friends. She has been especially close to Peter and MJ since the death of her close friend, May, and her years of experience and wisdom have helped the young couple through the loss of such a strong and loving influence in their lives.

--YOU CAN B ON THE PLANE ...IN

ANNA WATSON

Possessing nothing in the way of super powers except the power of the press and popular opinion, Daily Bugle publisher J. Jonah Jameson is nonetheless to be counted among Spider-Man's greatest nemeses. Ironically, however, he is also the man chiefly responsible for the livelihood of the man behind Spider-Man's mask: freelance photographer Peter Parker!

While still a high school student, Peter decided to photograph himself in action as Spider-Man and sell the photos to a newspaper. The blustery, curmudgeonly Jameson bought the photos, but much to Peter's chagrin, used them to perpetuate his rabid anti-Spider-Man editorial stance—a status quo that continues to this day, and continues to complicate Spider-Man's crimefighting career in New York.

Once a young, crusading reporter, Jameson has instilled his employees and his paper with a strong sense of journalistic ethics, retaining only one blind spot—Spider-Man. Jameson persists in his persecution of the wall-crawler as a dangerous vigilante despite many years of evidence to the contrary, and the Daily Bugle continues to be Peter Parker's chief source of income. After years of being its editor in chief and publisher, Jameson is now the owner of the Bugle as well, and shows no signs of abating in his ongoing campaign against Spider-Man.

J. JONAH JAMESON

FRIENDS OF SPIDER-MAN

Oh, WELL... J. JOHAH JAMESON, OUR ESTEEMED PUBLISHER, AWAITS.

JOE "ROBBIE" ROBERTSON

The Daily Bugle's "good cop" to J. Jonah Jameson's "bad cop", Joe "Robbie" Robertson began his career as the Bugle's city editor and later became its editor in chief. More importantly, Robbie has functioned as a conscience for his sometimes impulsive superior, Jameson, and as a friend and confidant to Peter Parker. In direct contrast to Jameson's usually antagonistic relationship with Peter, Robbie has lent an often-needed sympathetic ear to the young man's troubles, and has helped steer Peter toward honing his craft of photography.

A bastion of journalistic integrity, Joe Robertson has one dark secret in his past: his childhood friendship with the villain called Tombstone, and the fear of him which led to years of Robbie's keeping quiet about Tombstone's numerous crimes. Robbie has since pleaded guilty to these charges and served a harrowing jail term, after which he was released to his loving family and his friends at the Bugle, a stronger man for the experience. He continues to guide the daily Bugle's editorial staff and provide a calming, rationalizing influence on the ill-tempered Jonah Jameson.

When shy young photographer Peter Parker met Jonah Jameson's pretty secretary Betty Brant, it was puppy love at first sight. Betty was Peter's first love, and much of his early exploits as Spider-Man were plagued by Peter's insecurities and doubts regarding his relationship with this similarly shy young woman. Unfortunately, as fate would have it, Peter's double life did indeed impact on the fledgling relationship, and Betty found herself swept away in the arms of a dashing young reporter named Ned Leeds, the man she would later marry.

In later years, Peter and Betty would build a strong friendship from the remains of their young love, and it would prove to be a strong bond indeed. Peter was there when Ned Leeds was tragically killed on an assignment, and it was later erroneously revealed that he was leading a secret life as the costumed criminal called the Hobgoblin. Betty has picked up the pieces of her life admirably, and is now herself a reporter for the Bugle. She and Peter are still close, though her longstanding dislike and distrust of his alter ego Spider-Man remains as well.

BETTY BRANT LEEDS

FRIENDS OF SPIDER-MAN

When Peter Parker's early exploits as Spider-Man began affecting his already shaky relationship with Betty Brant, the pretty young secretary turned to the arms of this dashing, cosmopolitan young reporter for the Daily Bugle. Ned Leeds was everything that the insecure Parker believed he was not—the kind of man who could give Betty everything she deserved. For a long time, however, Betty still harbored feelings toward Peter, which led to a longstanding rivalry between the two. These feelings of enmity and jealousy eventually softened into a good professional working relationship between the hungry young journalist and the daring young photographer, and Ned's dangerous assignments often led him into situations wherein he had to be rescued by Peter's web-slinging alter ego.

Ned and Betty eventually married, and initially their life together was blissful. But Ned's ever-increasing obsessive dedication to his job led to his being away from home for longer and longer periods, which put a strain on the marriage and also led Ned into the assignment that would ultimately cost him his life: his expose on the supercriminal called the Hobgoblin. The Hobgoblin used his great resources to uncover Ned's investigation and then brainwash him to use as a sleeper agent and decoy. In Germany, Ned was manipulated by the real Hobgoblin into posing as the villain in a hotel room, where he was murdered by agents of the assassin called the Foreigner.

Only recently has the truth come out, and Ned's name been cleared of the crimes the Hobgoblin was accused of. At the very least, Betty can now rest easy knowing that her husband did not die as the evil man the Hobgoblin tried to make the world believe he had become.

NED LEEDS

FLASH THOMPSON

Another ironic facet of Spider-Man's early career was the fact that the president of Spider-Man's fan club was also the high school tormentor of Spidey's true identity, Peter Parker! The shy, bookish Parker proved an easy target for the jeers and practical jokes of football hero Flash, and it was all Peter could do not to use his amazing spider-powers for some sweet retaliation!

As both Peter and Flash graduated high school, and their future careers as collegians became imminent, their antagonistic relationship began to soften, and would abate further with Flash's tour of army duty overseas. But Flash's fortunes took a turn for the worse when he was framed by the Hobgoblin and imprisoned, and worse still when he was used by Spider-Man's ex-girlfriend Felicia Hardy as a suitor to make Peter jealous.

Now Flash is trying to pull his life together, attempting to prove to himself and his friends that his life didn't peak in his high school glory days. His admiration of Spider-Man remains strong, and may help pull him through these tough times.

FRIENDS OF SPIDER-MAN

A chain-smoking, cynical, hard-bitten reporter in the classic mold, Ben Urich provides a contrast to the idealistic young freelance photographer Peter Parker. Often partnered on dangerous assignments for the Daily Bugle, the two have grown to have a grudging respect for the skills, foibles, and worldview of each other, and hence have been successful in garnering many important crime exposes for their boss, J. Jonah Jameson.

Already a winner of the prestigious Pulitzer Prize for excellence in journalism, Ben Urich is always looking for the next big story, which brings him into the midst of dangerous, often life-threatening situations. As a result, Ben has also encountered Peter's costumed alter ego Spider-Man on numerous occasions. Though possessed of a reporter's natural curiosity, Ben has not delved deeply into discovering Spider-Man's true identity — a fact which certainly has Peter Parker sleeping more soundly at night!

Most recently, Peter and Ben have been conducting an investigation into the criminal empire of the mysterious European crimelord, Fortunato, who has gained a stranglehold on New York City's organized crime organizations. Once again, Ben Urich is treading dangerous ground in pursuit of another award-winning story.

PETER.

BEN URICH

GWEN STACY

The first great love of Peter Parker's life, Gwendolyn Stacy also proved to be the most tragic. Gwen met Peter in their early days of college, and took an instant liking to the quiet, sensitive science major. Peter was also attracted to Gwen, but a combination of insecurities, other romantic entanglements, and the constant distractions and dangers of his life as Spider-Man ensured that their relationship would not be an easy one to kindle or maintain. When Peter and Gwen finally did realize their true feelings for each other, and started a relationship, it was the first truly happy time in Peter Parker's troubled young life, and as fate would have it, it was not destined to last.

Spider-Man's insane archfoe the Green Goblin had discovered Parker's true identity, and was determined to destroy his web-slinging enemy in every way —physically, mentally, and emotionally. He accomplished the latter objective in a brutal, horrifying manner: he kidnapped the innocent Gwen, and threw her from the top of a bridge. Though Spider-Man managed to catch her before impact with the water below, the shock of the fall had already killed her. An enraged Spider-Man pursued the Goblin, determined to make him pay. The battle was fast and furious, and ultimately the Goblin ended up seemingly causing his own death in the course of the conflict.

Though now happily married to Mary Jane Watson, the death of Gwen Stacy still has a profound emotional impact on Peter Parker, and remains a constant reminder of the dangers associated with being a loved one of Spider-Man.

FRIENDS OF SPIDER-MAN

Since he appeared on the scene in New York City, the amazing Spider-Man's relationship with the police department has been shaky at best. Most cops, due to influences such as J. Jonah Jameson's Daily Bugle editorials, consider the web-slinging crimefighter a criminal himself. Captain George Stacy, conversely, was Spider-Man's first friend on the police force. Ironically, Stacy was also the father of Gwen Stacy, the girlfriend of Spider-Man's alter ego, Peter Parker.

Captain Stacy approved of his daughter's boyfriend Peter, thinking him to be a fine young man. At the same time, the Captain was curious about the secret identity of Spider-Man, and was actively investigating the wall-crawler while at the same time condoning his actions. He suspected a link between the shy young photographer and Spider-Man due to Peter's constantly managing to get news photos of Spidey's exploits. Later, Peter confessed to being Spider-Man in front of him while delirious from illness. Captain Stacy never got a chance to pursue the situation much further, as he was soon after killed while saving an innocent child from falling debris in a battle between Spider-Man and Dr. Octopus. Gwen blamed Spider-Man for her father's death, and thus, Peter was unable to tell her about his dual identity right up until her own tragic death.

Recently, George Stacy's brother Arthur, the head of a private investigation firm, moved from Hong Kong to America, where he intends to conduct a full investigation of Spider-Man and the role he played in the deaths of his brother and niece.

CAPT. GEORGE STACY

Peter Parker's best friend in college, Harry Osborn was always a very troubled young man. Harry's mental problems stemmed back to his childhood as the only son of Norman Osborn, the wealthy, ruthless industrialist who was also secretly the costumed criminal called the Green Goblin. Norman was a harsh, domineering father figure who never felt that Harry measured up to his expectations, and was not afraid to let Harry know it. The results were profound, deep-seated psychological problems of inadequacy, buried resentment, and a driving need to please his father.

Harry found solace from these problems in his friendship with Peter Parker — the young man whose alter ego was Norman's most hated enemy — and his romance with, and later marriage to, fellow student Liz Allan. At one point, Harry felt he needed more than his personal relationships to deal with his problems and turned to drugs, which led to a near-fatal overdose. Fortunately, Peter and others managed to help him through this crisis, and later bouts with madness when he took over his father's legacy as the Green Goblin after Norman's death.

However, the damage to Harry's fragile psyche had been done, and when he once again lapsed into his Green Goblin persona in recent years, Spider-Man's best efforts to cure his former best friend of the madness infecting him were not enough. The experimental strength-enhancing formula Harry used on himself as the Goblin eventually took his life. He leaves behind a widow, Liz, and a son, Norman II, whom Liz prays can avoid falling victim to the Osborn legacy of madness.

HARRY OSBORN

FRIENDS OF SPIDER-MAN

LIZ ALLAN OSBORN

Liz Allan was initially nothing more to Peter Parker than yet another member of the popular crowd that had nothing but disdain for the studious, introverted young man. But Liz later saw something more in Peter, and became his defender against the insults and pranks of Flash Thompson and his ilk. Unfortunately, this act of kindness ultimately made things worse, as Flash had a long-standing crush on Liz, while Liz was finding herself more and more attracted to Peter.

While Peter and Liz never really became an item, they remained good friends throughout high school and college, and Liz eventually met and became romantically involved with Peter's college roommate Harry Osborn. Harry and Liz were eventually married, and Liz gave birth to their first child, Norman II. The Osborns' marriage, though tranquil on the surface, was always haunted by the spectre of Harry's father Norman, the original Green Goblin, and the effect he had on Harry's mental state. Several times, Harry adopted the identity of the Goblin, only to be thwarted in his schemes and returned to seeming normalcy by Peter's alter ego, Spider-Man.

Harry's most recent bout with madness cost him his life, leaving Liz a very young widow, and also the heir apparent to the Osborn company and family fortune. Liz now runs Osborn Chemicals with the aid of her half-brother, Mark Raxton (the reformed criminal once known as the Molten Man), while raising her son, little Norman.

The son of bombastic Daily Bugle publisher J. Jonah Jameson, John has been both trusted friend and vicious foe to Spider-Man throughout his career. Spider-Man met John Jameson — at the time a young astronaut — in his very early days as a hero, saving his life from the crash of an experimental manned space probe. This rescue gained Spidey the gratitude of John, but the ire of Jonah Jameson, who saw it as the glory-seeking web-slinger stealing his son's thunder.

Later, John's space travels brought him into contact with strange forces that disrupted his life. A gem that John brought back to Earth mutated him into a werewolf-like creature known as the Man-Wolf. Spider-Man battled the Man-Wolf, stopping its rampage, and eventually managed to help John Jameson revert back to his human self. The Man-Wolf persona resurrected itself several times over the years, but Spider-Man, much to Jonah Jameson's chagrin, has always been instrumental in curing his son of the space gem's affliction. With the destruction of the gem after their most recent encounter, John seems to be permanently cured of being the Man-Wolf.

John has taken a job as Chief of Security at Ravencroft Institute, the psychiatric facility that contains several super-powered patients. In this capacity, his body was once again mutated by an outside source — the psychotic symbiote of the serial killer Carnage. Jameson was cured once again, however, and maintains both his security job and his friendship with the web-slinger.

JOHN JAMESON

MAYBE--

--MAYBE I'D BETTER TAKE YOU TO HER.

FRIENDS OF SPIDER-MAN

DR. ASHLEY KAFKA

A dedicated psychologist, sometimes to the point of fanaticism, Dr. Ashley Kafka is the head of the Ravencroft Institute for the Criminally Insane, plying her trade toward the goal of curing some of the world's most dangerous super-powered psychopaths. In this capacity, she has come into contact with Spider-Man several times, and has found that the wall-crawling hero himself occasionally has need of her expertise and sympathetic ear.

Some of the patients incarcerated at the Institute that Dr. Kafka has aided include the second Carrion, Shriek, the Chameleon, and Edward Whelan, formerly known as Vermin. Some patients, however, have eluded curing despite Dr. Kafka's best efforts, including the late Harry Osborn, the second Green Goblin, who was a temporary inmate of Ravencroft; the Jackal, who actually managed to break out of the Institute before his therapy could advance; and Ravencroft's most dangerous inmate, Carnage, whom even the altruistic Kafka is starting to believe may be incurable.

Dr. Kafka has not given up, however, and continues her dedicated efforts to rehabilitate some of the world's most notorious villains, while lending advice and a helping hand to the man who put many of them away: Spider-Man.

GREEN GOBLIN I

The greatest of all of Spidey's foes, no one has done more to wreck the web-slinger's life than the original Green Goblin!

Experimenting with a secret formula that would enhance his strength, ruthless industrialist Norman Osborn didn't realize that exposure to the chemical would also drive him completely insane. And so was born the Green Goblin—a cackling, crazed criminal genius whose obsession was to destroy Spider-Man! Outfitting himself with pumpkin bombs, electricity-blasting gloves and an amazing goblin-glider, the Green Goblin attacked Spider-Man mercilessly, even discovering Spidey's true identity at one point. All that prevented Norman from realizing his murderous goal was a bout of amnesia, which hid all memory of his Green Goblin persona.

But Norman's sanity didn't last, and once again the Green Goblin soared the skies of New York City in search of Spider-Man, with tragic results. In an attempt to lure Spidey into a final showdown with him, the Goblin kidnapped Spidey's then-girlfriend, Gwen Stacy. Despite Spider-Man's best efforts, the Goblin took Gwen's life—sending her hurtling off the top of a bridge. In the aftermath of the ensuing battle with Spidey, the Goblin himself was killed, impaled by his own glider— or so Spidey thought.

Only recently did Spidey discover that Norman had survived, kept alive by the mysterious Goblin formula. Secretly moving to Europe, Norman built a sprawling, secretive criminal empire. But the death of his son, Harry, Norman's successor as the Green Goblin, brought him back to the States for one final act of revenge against his nemesis! Wielding his evil influence to convince Peter Parker that he was really a clone, the Goblin eventually killed the cloned version of Peter that had replaced Parker as Spider-Man!

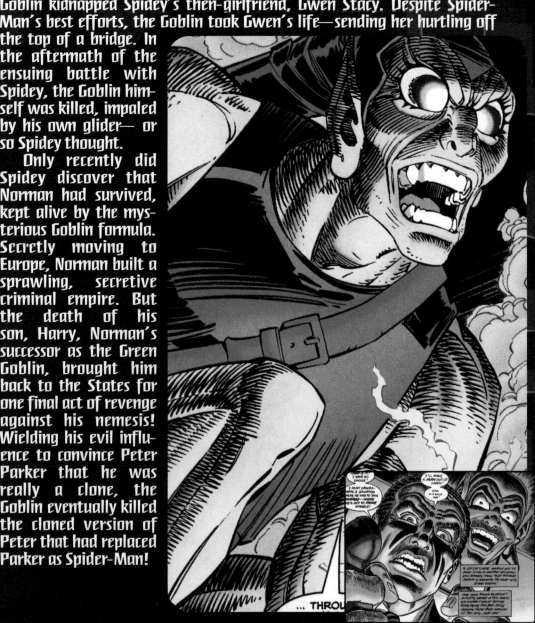

DOCTOR OCTOPUS I

With a whirl of bone-crushing steel tentacles at his command, the late Doctor Octopus has proven to be one of Spider-Man's deadliest enemies.

Once he was Otto Octavius, a brilliant and respected scientist who had designed a set of robotic arms to aid in his atomic physics research. But a freak laboratory accident exposed Octavius to intense radioactivity, grafting his mechanical appendages to his body and giving him complete telepathic control over them. And worst of all, the accident altered his mind, turning him from a timid physicist into a criminally insane megalomaniac.

Armed—quite literally—with four powerful and nearly indestructible tentacles, Octavius took the name Doctor Octopus and turned his genius to solely criminal pursuits. He formed gangs, built criminal empires and eventually even sought world domination. But one man repeatedly got in his way—Spider-Man!

Over the years, Doctor Octopus has shown himself to be one of Spider-Man's most formidable foes, and their battles have proven to be as brutal as any the web-slinger has ever fought. But it was not Spider-Man who was responsible for the Doctor's recent demise—it was Spidey's degenerate clone, Kaine. In an attempt to prevent his prophetic vision of Mary Jane Parker's death, Kaine took the extreme and ultimately misguided measure of killing as many of Spider-Man's enemies as he could, figuring that by ending their lives he would prevent them from endangering hers. Ironically, only moments before Kaine killed him, Doctor Octopus had just saved Spider-Man's life.

VENOM

Never has Spider-Man faced a more vicious mass of mayhem than the super-brute known as Venom. Infused with an intense hatred of the wall-crawler from the moment of his creation, Venom has tried to kill Spidey many times, even threatening to eat his brains!

Venom began as two separate beings: Eddie Brock, a human whose career as a reporter came to an abrupt end when Spider-Man unwittingly exposed a story of his as false; and an alien symbiote, which for a time posed as Spidey's black costume, until the wall-crawler realized it was actually alive and rejected it. A chance meeting allowed both beings to combine their separate hatreds for Spider-Man into one overwhelming animosity when they merged to form Venom.

Venom has all of Spider-Man's powers and even greater strength. He can disguise himself to look like anything he can imagine, and he doesn't trigger Spider-Man's protective spider-sense. Luckily for Spidey, loud noises can shred the symbiote right off Eddie's back, and fire can hurt them as well.

Many innocent people have died, victims of Venom's bloodthirsty obsession to kill Spider-Man. But recently Venom has reformed himself, realizing that, like Spider-Man, he must use his powers to help innocent people, not hurt them. So now he claims to be humanity's "lethal protector," saving his punishments only for those he deems guilty. And although a shaky truce now exists between him and Spidey, the wall-crawler knows better than to relax for even a second when Venom's in town.

CARNAGE

Never has a Spider-Man villain had a name more fitting—or more frightening! Spreading terror and death wherever he goes, Carnage wields his murderous might with a zest that can only come from one who is utterly depraved.

Even before he became Carnage, Cletus Kasady was a notorious serial killer. Locked away in prison, he ended up sharing a jail cell with Eddie Brock—the man otherwise known as Venom. When Brock escaped, the spawn of the symbiotic alien costume that gives Venom his powers got left behind—and bonded with Kasady, merging with his very blood and granting him super-strength. His body now a writhing mass of crimson tendrils and razor-sharp claws, Kasady became Carnage— and the world became a much more dangerous place for everyone else!

Carnage lives for chaos. He revels in the pain and suffering he inflicts on the innocent, and counts every senseless death he causes as a reason for celebration. Only Spider-Man's repeated, heroic efforts have prevented Carnage from taking an even greater toll on human life than he already has. But as long as symbiote-laced blood still flows within Kasady's veins, Carnage's next victim is only the flick of a razor-edged finger away.

JACKAL

As misguided a menace as Spider-Man ever faced, the Jackal turned his love for a woman he could never have into a hatred for a hero he ultimately could not beat.

The Jackal entered Spider-Man's life as Professor Miles Warren, Peter Parker's brilliant college biology teacher. Warren secretly loved Peter's then-girlfriend, Gwen Stacy. When Gwen died at the hands of the Green Goblin, Warren mistakenly blamed Spider-Man. His personality split in two—the lovestruck Warren and the evil Jackal. Obsessed with replacing Gwen, he cloned her from a cell sample he had taken from her prior to her death. He cloned Spider-Man as well, in an attempt to have the clone kill the true Spidey. Ultimately, he neither won the Gwen-clone's love nor killed Spidey, but his failures only made him more determined to take revenge on the wall-crawler.

His obsession turning to utter madness, he sought to replace all of mankind with clones. Using Spider-Man's cells as the basis for his experiments, he produced hundreds of clones, including Ben Reilly and Kaine. He also genetically altered himself, taking on the animal characteristics of a true jackal and enhancing his strength, agility and speed.

His twisted plans came to a climax when, under the secret manipulations of the first Green Goblin, he convinced the real Spider-Man that he was a clone, and manipulated Ben Reilly into replacing the wall-crawler. As Spider-Man and Ben were putting an end to his genocidal dreams, the Jackal accidentally fell to his death in one last, unsuccessful attempt to win the love of the clone of Gwen.

THE PUMA

One of Spider-Man's most relentless and savage adversaries, the man called the Puma was born Thomas Fireheart to an Indian tribe in the American Southwest, and groomed for a very special destiny. The end product of generations of controlled breeding and mystical rituals, Fireheart was the latest of his family line to be appointed the protector of his tribe against the coming of the omnipotent cosmic being known as the Beyonder. Though he disbelieved the legends of this coming threat, he dedicated himself to becoming the perfect warrior. He later entered the white man's world as both a corporate wheeler-dealer, and as one of the world's most feared and respected mercenaries.

It was as a mercenary that the Puma first came into contact with Spider-Man. Their first brutal conflict led to a longstanding feud between the two, which escalated when Thomas Fireheart, in his civilian guise as head of Fireheart Enterprises, bought the Daily Bugle and interfered with the personal life of Spidey's alter ego, Peter Parker in the process.

TOMBSTONE

A brutal lifelong criminal with a body as cold, hard, and unyielding as his name implies, the man called Tombstone was born Lonnie Lincoln. An albino, his skin color and a voice defect that caused him to speak only in whispers made him an outcast, and left him greatly embittered. He built his body to peak physical condition and turned to a life of crime, using his cruel childhood nickname "Tombstone" as an alias.

Tombstone's only friend growing up was Joe Robertson, now editor in chief of the Daily Bugle. After years as a hitman in Philadelphia, Tombstone came to New York

to make his mark on the crime scene. Robertson's fear of his former childhood acquaintance brought Spider-Man into conflict with Tombstone several times. During one of these encounters, accidental exposure to a new chemical compound endowed Tombstone with rock-hard skin and superhuman strength. Even though he was now more than a physical match for the web-slinger, Tombstone was again defeated and his efforts to control the New York underworld thwarted.

However, Tombstone remains a formidable presence in organized crime in New York, and continues to nurse his grudge against Spider-Man and Joe Robertson, the "best friend" whom he feels has betrayed him.

HAMMERHEAD

A throwback to 1920's gangsters, Hammerhead's outdated manner of speech and dress mask a truly dangerous and cagey criminal mastermind. A small-time gangster whose real name is unknown, even to himself, the man now known as Hammerhead was found beaten and amnesiac in an alley by criminal surgeon Jonas Harrow. Harrow saved the man's life by inserting a steel plate in his skull. The thug, fixating on a poster for an old-time gangster movie, decided to model himself after the criminal figures of that era. A combination of cunning, ruthlessness and the use of his steel skull as an offensive weapon took Hammerhead to the top of a prominent crime family.

Hammerhead began a gang war with the other major player in the underworld scene at the time—Dr. Octopus—and Spider-Man became involved in the conflict. The wall-crawling hero succeeded in bringing the war to a halt and stopping the schemes of both Octopus and Hammerhead. However, Hammerhead has returned on numerous occasions, always attempting to claw his way to the top of organized crime, but is consistently brought down in his efforts by Spider-Man.

Recently, Hammerhead attempted another takeover of the crime scene, only to be crushed by the mysterious European crimelord Fortunato, and pressed into his service as a lieutenant. Most likely, Hammerhead is plotting a mutiny against his despised superior.

THE ROSE

The Rose burst upon the New York crime scene several years ago, his face hidden behind a leather mask and his motivations a mystery. Spider-Man disrupted his criminal operations several times before the Rose decided to wage war in earnest upon the wall-crawler. His most ambitious campaign began when he joined forces with another of Spider-Man's foes, the original Hobgoblin, in an unholy alliance designed to bring about the webbed hero's destruction and to depose the Rose's then-superior, the Kingpin of Crime, from his throne as crimelord of New York City.

The reason for this master plan was evident when the Rose was unmasked as the Kingpin's own estranged son, Richard Fisk, who despised his father's criminal empire. The partnership between the Rose and the Hobgoblin did indeed prove mutually beneficial to both, and harmful to the Kingpin's operations. However, both ultimately failed to kill Spider-Man, and the partnership came to an abrupt end when the Hobgoblin was apparently killed and the Kingpin reasserted his control over his son and his empire.

Recently, another man calling himself the Rose has surfaced. This Rose claims not to be Richard Fisk, though his ambitions seem the same: the elimination of Spider-Man and the consolidation of power in the underworld.

KINGPIN

One of Spider-Man's most powerful and dangerous foes is a man who has no super powers or special abilities except his cunning criminal genius. Wilson Fisk, the Kingpin of Crime, started his rise to the top of the underworld from very humble beginnings. A poverty-stricken, tormented childhood led Fisk to intensely dedicate himself to the study of martial arts, physical conditioning, and the use of political and economic power. The result was that by the time he had reached adulthood, Fisk was the undisputed head of the most powerful and extensive crime family on the East Coast... and in position to brutally seize power from all the others to become the first true Kingpin of Crime.

Spider-Man's first encounter with the Kingpin began when the web-slinging hero had briefly retired from crimefighting. Hearing this news, the Kingpin decided the time had come for his master plan: to unite the various criminal gangs in New York City under his leadership, and conduct a crime wave such as the city had never seen. Fortunately, though the Kingpin was successful in consolidating his organization, Spider-Man's retirement proved to be a temporary one, and Spidey mangaed to put a stop to the crimewave.

This was but the first of many clashes between the obese crimelord and the heroic web-slinger. Spider-Man has countless times quashed the Kingpin's various schemes and defeated him and his pawns, but has never been able to imprison the Kingpin himself, or successfully charge him with any crimes. Building a number of legitimate businesses from his ill-gotten gains, including a spice company based in the far east, the Kingpin's public

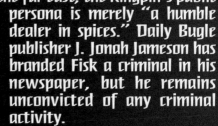

persona is merely "a humble dealer in spices." Daily Bugle publisher J. Jonah Jameson has branded Fisk a criminal in his newspaper, but he remains unconvicted of any criminal activity.

In recent times, the Kingpin has focused more of his attention on another enemy: Spidey's fellow crimefighter Daredevil. After years of conducting their private war, Daredevil has, with the aid of SHIELD and other factors, managed to topple the Kingpin from the top of the East Coast organized crime scene. The Kingpin has vowed to climb back up to the top, however, and the threat should not be taken lightly— for he has done it before!

RHINO

All that is known about the Rhino's early life is that he was a poor Russian immigrant, working as muscle for various criminal employers to support himself. At one point, he was hired by hostile foreign agents to undergo an experimental process that would transform him into an unstoppable, superhuman agent. The process involved bonding his skin to a super-tough, rhinoceros hide-like polymer bodysuit which greatly augmented his strength, endurance, and resistance to physical harm. The Rhino's first mission brought him into battle with Spider-Man, who prevailed against the horned villain after a hard-fought battle.

The Rhino has returned time and again to pursue his goals as a hired criminal, and to renew his vengeful vendetta against Spider-Man. The Rhino has also gone up against such foes as the Hulk, the Thing, Iron Man, and, more recently, the new, heroic Green Goblin. He has also, on occasion, joined forces with other costumed criminals, such as the Sinister Syndicate and the Emissaries of Evil.

When last seen, the Rhino had hired his services as a player in the super-powered gladiatorial contest known as the Great Game, and met defeat at the hands of Kaine. The Rhino never seems to stay incarcerated for long, however, and he will most likely be charging into Spider-Man's life when the web-slinger least expects it!

THIS AIN'T PERSONAL PEOPLE!

THE SHOCKER

The Shocker began his criminal career as an unsuccessful burglar named Herman Schultz... and though his thieving skills left much to be desired, his aptitude with mechanical devices was a force to be reckoned with! Serving a jail term, Schultz finagled a job in the prison workshop, wherein he cobbled together a crude safe-cracking device that emitted destructive vibratory waves. This "vibro-shock" device enabled him to escape captivity and begin a new and far more effective crime spree. Fitting the "vibro-shock" technology into wrist-mounted units, Schultz dubbed himself the Shocker, and embarked on a series of thefts that brought him into conflict with the amazing Spider-Man.

Still a burglar at heart, the Shocker has seldom used his invention for much more than stealing, though he has occasionally taken on assignments as an assassin and has been a member of several criminal organizations, including the Masters of Evil. However, his efforts have been thwarted time and again by one costumed crimefighter or another, despite making improvements over the years to his suit's vibratory powers. His latest campaign—an attempt to collect a bounty on Spider-Man—has once again landed the Shocker in prison, where he plots revenge and his next big score.

BEETLE

This high-flying fiend has gone up against several super heroes over the years, but no one has had the misfortune to fight him more often than Spider-Man. And although the Beetle hasn't had the greatest of successes against Spidey, he's been one of the most persistent pests ever to bug the wall-crawler.

Before he became the Beetle, Abner Jenkins was a disgruntled, underpaid mechanic at an airline parts factory. Deciding it was time for a career change, he applied his mechanical mastery to building an armor-plated

Beetle suit and embarked on a life of crime. From the time of his debut battle with the Human Torch until today, he's continued to modify and improve his suit, making it one of the most formidable weapons Spidey has ever faced: it flies up to 100 mph, is impervious to most bullets and other projectiles, gives Abner super-strength, and can discharge powerful electrostatic blasts—electro-bites—through the fingertips of its gloves.

Combining his formidable battlesuit with his sheer inventive brilliance, the Beetle continues to buzz Spider-Man much too closely for the wall-crawler's comfort.

HYDRO-MAN

Always a threat to dampen Spider-Man's spirits, Hydro-Man has made quite a splash since he arrived on the crime scene.

As Morrie Bench, cargo ship crewman, a freak accident exposed him to an experimental generator, seawater and volcanic gases. These elements combined to alter his body, giving Bench the ability to transform himself into a liquid substance resembling water. With absolute control of every droplet within him, Bench quickly learned how to use his power in all sorts of ways, including shooting high-pressure jets of liquid powerful enough to collapse the side of a building.

SPEAKING OF WHOM: SOME 1,500 MILES AWAY...

THIS ISN'T DODGE CITY IN THE 1800's, HYDRO-MAN!

Despite his super-villainous credentials, Hydro-Man is still a small-time thug at heart, and not a very smart one at that. Still, although he may lack the steel-hard sinews of some of Spidey's other enemies, he's still one of the toughest foes the wall-crawler has ever had to face.

SCORPION

With a cybernetic steel tail that can shoot powerful energy blasts and crush a car with a mere flick of its tip, the Scorpion packs a sting that Spider-Man has spent more time avoiding than he'd care to remember.

The Scorpion started out as private investigator Mac Gargan, originally hired by Daily Bugle publisher J. Jonah Jameson to discover how Peter Parker managed to score so many exclusive photographs of Spider-Man. But soon, after Jameson paid him an additional $10,000, Gargan agreed to undergo a treatment that would give him the power to defeat Spider-Man. Unfortunately, the treatment also had the unexpected side-effect of turning him into a psychotic, and so was born the Scorpion.

The Scorpion possesses superhuman strength, speed, agility and endurance, abilities he's employed throughout his long criminal career to get what he wants. But what he wants most are the deaths of Spider-Man and his former employer, Jameson—two goals that have so far eluded him. Ironically, Spidey has had to save Jameson several times from the Scorpion.

RRRRRRRR

KRAVEN THE HUNTER

Born Sergei Kravinoff, this only son of Russian aristocrats grew up to become Kraven, the greatest big game hunter in the world. After running out of challenges among the animal kingdom, he sought one more trophy to add to his collection—Spider-Man!

Originally summoned to America by the Chameleon to hunt Spidey, Kraven's initial failure to bring down his superhuman prey made him grow obsessed with defeating the wall-crawler. Over the years, abetted by his own superhuman strength, speed, agility and stamina, Kraven employed various primitive weapons and natural poisons to fight Spider-Man. With a ferocity matching that of the wild beasts he stalked, Kraven was one of the most dangerous opponents Spidey ever faced. After numerous battles, Kraven finally succeeded in defeating the wall-crawler, burying him alive on the hunter's estate. Satisfied with his triumph and with no other challenges worthy of him in the offing, Kraven decided to end his own life.

But even death did not end their conflict. In a trial-by-combat to ransom the soul of Kraven, Spider-Man had to fight one final battle—with Kraven's re-animated corpse! Spidey triumphed, and Kraven's soul was saved.

VERMIN

Edward Whelan escaped from a childhood of abuse and neglect into the harsh, unforgiving streets of New York. He eked out a pitiful existence until he was lured away by agents of the insidious Baron Zemo and forced to take part in a horrid genetics experiment. The frightened Whelan was transformed by the Baron's super-science into the man-rat known as Vermin. Vermin possessed the ability to control rats, as well as ratlike attributes, such as razor-sharp teeth and claws, and superhuman strength, speed and agility.

Vermin's first foe, as per Zemo's command, was the Baron's enemy, Captain America. After meeting with defeat and imprisonment in that encounter, Vermin broke free of confinement and went on a savage, cannibalistic reign of terror in Manhattan. But his killing spree was brutally cut short by Kraven the Hunter, who at the time was masquerading as Spider-Man. When the real Spider-Man returned, he freed Vermin from Kraven's torturous captivity and helped him into the hands of much-needed psychiatric help.

Now, through the aid of Spider-Man and psychologist Dr. Ashley Kafka, Vermin has faced his inner demons, and has even reverted back to his human form as Edward Whelan. His Vermin identity seems to be permanently buried in Whelan's subconscious, but whether Spidey has truly seen the last of this chilling menace remains to be seen!

CHAMELEON

He's a man of a thousand faces—and none of them are his own! Dmitri Smerdyakov began his criminal career as an international spy working for a hostile world power. As part of his training, he became a master of disguise, able to create lifelike masks and mimic virtually any voice. Recently, he improved on his already formidable talents when he acquired the ability to make his flesh malleable, giving him the power to almost instantly transform his features to look like anybody else's.

Spider-Man first battled the Chameleon very early in his career, and since then they've crossed paths many times. The two have clashed while the Chameleon has engaged in numerous covert operations, masterminded spectacular thefts, allied himself with various criminal organizations and even tried to climb to the top of New York City's criminal underworld. Realizing early on that Spider-Man was the chief obstacle to his illicit ambitions, the Chameleon has often employed others to carry out his war against the web-slinger.

The most telling blow the Chameleon has ever landed on his arch-enemy was not physical, but emotional. He manipulated Peter Parker into believing that his parents, who were thought to be dead, had returned. The shock of learning the truth—that the Chameleon had fooled him with artificial beings in his parents' place—was as devastating as any defeat Spider-Man has ever suffered.

GREEN GOBLIN II

No foe of Spider-Man's has tested the web-slinger's resolve more than the second Green Goblin—for beneath the maniacal mask was none other than Peter Parker's best friend, Harry Osborn!

Blaming Spider-Man for the supposed death of his father, Harry succumbed to the madness that is the Osborn family's sad legacy and became the Green Goblin in his place. With all the weaponry and powers of the original Goblin at his disposal, Harry cast aside his friendship with Peter and vowed to avenge Norman Osborn's death— by killing Spider-Man.

And he almost succeeded. For months he menaced Spidey's friends and family. And in a final battle, the second Green Goblin seemed about to succeed where the first had failed. But the last-minute return of his sanity spurred the Green Goblin to rescue Spidey from the trap he had set for him. And the battle had another, far more tragic result: the experimental strength-enhancing serum Harry had taken proved to be more than his body could handle, and took his life.

DR. OCTOPUS II

When Otto Octavius, the first Doctor Octopus, was killed, Spider-Man thought that the evil of his eight-limbed archfoe would perish with him. Unfortunately, such was not to be the case. Octavius had a protege— an ambitious and embittered young woman named Carolyn Trainer—whose obsession with science and controlling the information networks of the world led her to assume the mantle of Dr. Octopus after her mentor's death.

The new Doctor Octopus encountered Spider-Man while attempting to kidnap her estranged father Seward Trainer, an acquaintance of Spider-Man's whom she thought would hold the knowledge of his secrets. She was defeated in this initial encounter, but Spider-Man soon discovered that her resources were far beyond those possessed by the original Doc Ock. The new Doctor Octopus is the leader of a far-reaching organization called the Network, and her mysterious partner in her criminal endeavors is an evil entity known only as the Master Programmer, a being who exists only in cyberspace. Doc Ock and the Programmer set in motion a master plan to merge our reality with the Programmer's unique virtual reality dimension, but this was foiled by Spider-Man's ally, the Scarlet Spider, and the Master Programmer's essence was scattered into the ether.

Doctor Octopus returned to once again attempt to kidnap her father, but was defeated and sent to prison by the second Spider-Man, Ben Reilly. The state of her organization is at the moment unknown.

THE VULTURE

The criminal career of the Vulture began when Adrian Toomes, an electronics engineer and partner in the small firm of Bestman and Toomes, discovered that his partner, Gregory Bestman, was stealing his share of the company profits. At the time, Toomes' major project was an electronic harness that would enable the wearer to fly. Toomes later discovered that the electromagnetic energy in the harness also granted the user superhuman strength. When he threatened Bestman, Toomes was shocked to discover that all the company's assets were in his partner's name and he was thrown out of the firm. Already elderly and now deeply embittered, Toomes perfected his flying harness and created the identity of the Vulture to terrorize his former partner and destroy his business.

The Vulture soon discovered the thrill of using his flight and strength powers for crime, and began a spree of robberies in New York City that brought the then-fledgling crimefighter Spider-Man onto his trail. Spider-Man managed to defeat the Vulture and end his crime wave, but the Vulture has repeatedly escaped from imprisonment over the years, concerned with his main goals of wealth through illegal means and revenge on the web-slinger.

While in prison, the Vulture discovered that the energy in the harness that gave him his super-strength had also given him terminal cancer. To settle accounts before his death, this time he went on a murder spree, killing Bestman and others whom he felt had wronged Adrian Toomes during his lifetime. He was again stopped and captured by Spider-Man. Later, the Vulture learned of a device called the Juvenator, which could drain the life energy from one human being and use it to rejuvenate the damaged cells of another. The Vulture stole the device and used it to inadvertently drain the life force from the artificial being that was posing as Peter Parker's mother. The result was an almost vampiric Vulture with no discernible human emotions, and the need to retain his artificial youth by draining the life energy of his victims.

ELECTRO

Electro packs enough power within his body to light up a small city like it was Times Square on a Saturday night. Lucky for Spider-Man that this career criminal's intelligence doesn't shine with anywhere near the same intensity.

A freak accident launched Electro on his life of crime when, as Maxwell Dillon, he was struck by lightning while working as a high-wire lineman for the power company. The blast infused him with the ability to discharge massive bolts of electricity, which Dillon quickly applied to strictly criminal pursuits.

By himself and allied with other super-villains, Electro has encountered Spider-Man on many occasions. But despite his best efforts to turn the web-swinger into a web-cinder, Electro has met defeat repeatedly. Failure, however, has not deterred him: Electro remains determined to give Spider-Man the shock of his life!

THE LIZARD

Dr. Curtis Connors was an army surgeon who lost his right arm while in the service. Also a brilliant herpetologist, Connors became convinced that his studies into the regenerative abilities of certain reptiles could be applied to human physiology to help him to regrow his lost arm. Isolating the reptile enzymes that stimulated regrowth, he created an experimental serum with which he injected himself. Unfortunately, though the serum did indeed restore his missing arm, it also triggered a horrific body-wide mutation which transformed the hapless scientist into a savage, humanoid reptile being which called itself the Lizard.

Possessed of a primitive but cunning reptilian mind, the Lizard intended to gather a reptile army that would supplant humanity as the ruling species on Earth. He was stopped in his scheme by Spider-Man, who used Connors' chemicals and his own scientific knowledge to create a serum that reversed the effects of the original formula, returning the Lizard to his human identity. However, the effects of the original serum remained in Connors' genetic make-up, and to this day, though he has gone long periods without trans- forming to his reptilian alter ego, he has never been able to fully free himself from the curse of the Lizard. Spider-Man, in both his costumed and civilian identities, has remained a trusted friend of Curt Connors and his family, and often helped them through their various dealings with the Lizard.

Recently, Connors' latest attempt to cure himself from his transformations led an over-anxious lab assistant to inject some of the Lizard's DNA into a discarded piece of the Lizard's severed tail. The tail then grew into an even more animalistic and mindless version of the Lizard, which was mistaken for the true Lizard for months. In actuality, this monstrous Lizard was searching for Connors, driven by a primal need for Connors' human side to make it whole. The monster Lizard finally caught up with Connors and his son. To save his child, Connors injected himself again with the Lizard serum, and the original Lizard fought a battle to the death with the monster Lizard. Spider-Man became involved in the battle, and once again put a halt to the original Lizard's schemes. But the Lizard's persona seems to be awake in the subconscious of Curt Connors, and hinting at a larger agenda for the world and humanity than before. It remains to be seen if these schemes come to fruition.

HOBGOBLIN

Much about the Hobgoblin remains unrevealed, but there's no hiding the fact that he's one especially vicious criminal. Robbery, blackmail and kidnapping are just a few of his favorite pastimes. And for the right price he'll happily hire himself out to do the dirty work of others.

The man behind the Hobgoblin's mask began his illicit career when he uncovered a hidden lair of the original Green Goblin and systematically looted that and other lairs as well. Acquiring the strength-enhancing Goblin serum and an arsenal consisting of a flying, rocket-powered bat glider, pumpkin bombs, blaster gloves and razor-edged throwing bats, this mysterious thief took the name Hobgoblin. He quickly discovered he had acquired something else of the Green Goblin's: Spider-Man as his arch-enemy.

Over the years, others have assumed the Hobgoblin identity, most notably the mercenary Jason Macendale. But no matter who has worn the costume, they all share with the original a virtually unbroken record of losing to Spider-Man in battle.

Although the original Hobgoblin recently returned to murder the Macendale Hobgoblin, his true identity is still unknown. Unfortunately for Spider-Man and the rest of the law-abiding public, his criminal intent is all too clear.

MYSTERIO

Mysterio is a master of special effects who long ago chose law-breaking over movie-making. Starting out as Quentin Beck, Hollywood stuntman, he became fascinated with Spider-Man and the idea of using his special-effects skills to duplicate the wall-crawler's feats. But fascination turned to failure when he tried unsuccessfully to discredit Spidey.

Since then, Mysterio's career path has turned sharply criminal. He craves fame and fortune, but sees no point in working toward either goal honestly. He uses a variety of tricks—lasers, artificial fog, hypnotism, chemical hallucinogens, explosives—to commit his crimes and keep Spider-Man off-balance. Although some of his assaults on Spidey have bordered on sheer genius, Mysterio is smart enough to know that it will take much more than smoke and mirrors to permanently defeat the wall-crawler.

TENDRIL

One of Spider-Man's newest and most horrific foes, the web-slinger's own scientific research is partially responsible for the creation of the monster called Tendril. After receiving the test results that told him he was a clone (later proven to be false), Peter Parker moved from New York to Portland, Oregon with his wife Mary Jane, intending to start a new, normal life there and begin a family. Peter took a job at Galaman Research, the company that originally conducted the demonstration wherein Peter received his spider-powers. Peter ran tests on his own physiology, hoping to learn more about the origin of his abilities. Samples of irradiated blood from Peter's body were later used, without Peter's consent, to treat a patient named River Verys for a skin disease called Necrotizing Fascitis. The result was that Verys mutated into a creature whose skin was made up of strands of organic webbing—Tendril.

Peter, at this point retired as Spider-Man, once again donned his costume, feeling responsible for Tendril's creation. Spider-Man and Tendril clashed, with the villain successfully making an escape at first. Their second clash also involved another Necrotizing Fascitis victim, called Dryrot. Both were captured and exposed to a radiation treatment that would cure their affliction, but Verys, unwilling to surrender his powers, fought the treatment, and ultimately died. As a result of his exposure to the treatment, Peter Parker himself lost his Spider-Man powers, which have only recently returned.

KAINE

A brutal, grim reflection of everyone's favorite web-slinger, Kaine has the dubious honor of being the very first Spider-Man clone. Unfortunately for him, his creator, the Jackal, had not perfected his cloning technique yet—not even close. Instead, Kaine's birthright included all of Spider-Man's great powers but little of his sense of responsibility. Deemed a failure by his maker, Kaine was cast out by the Jackal. Add the fact that Kaine's flesh suffers from an apparently irreversible degeneration that has left his body horribly scarred, it's no wonder why Kaine is the pathetic mess of a man he is today.

Driven by jealousy and hatred, Kaine spent years stalking Ben Reilly, the clone that the Jackal had perfected, doing everything in his power to make Ben's life miserable. In many cases, those who crossed him died by his hand. Among his victims were the original Doctor Octopus and Kraven's son, the Grim Hunter—killed because of Kaine's misguided efforts to protect Mary Jane Watson-Parker from being murdered. Others suffered the Mark of Kaine, a searing brand that Kaine left on his victims' faces with the touch of his palm.

Wracked by guilt and self-pity, Kaine recently tried to force Ben to kill him, but without success. Instead, inspired by Ben's example, Kaine turned himself in to the authorities to pay for his crimes. It remains to be seen whether his remorse is permanent or if he'll return to his murderous ways.

GAUNT

Little did Spider-Man realize when he fought a minor foe called the Robot Master in the early days of his career that that foe would turn out to be a player in a master plan that nearly destroyed his life. Mendel Stromm was the business partner of Norman Osborn, the industrialist who would later become the Green Goblin. Stromm was borrowing funds from the company with the intent of repaying them, but when Norman discovered this, he used the opportunity to have Stromm arrested for embezzlement. Norman later stole all of Stromm's inventions and chemical innovations, using them to forge his Green Goblin identity.

Stromm emerged from prison years later, bent on revenge on his former partner— and possessing the brilliant knowledge of robotics to implement it. Stromm sent a cadre of super-advanced robots after Osborn, but was unsuccessful in killing him due to the interference of Spider-Man, who was at that point unaware of Norman's double identity as the Green Goblin. Stromm himself apparently dropped dead of a heart attack, but very recently, this seeming "death" played into a far grander agenda.

In actuality, Stromm had earlier injected himself with a crude version of the strength-enhancing formula later used by the Green Goblin. The formula preserved Stromm's life within his tomb, though his body decayed into a gaunt, frail, corpse-like state. His still-functioning body was exhumed by his hated former employer, Norman Osborn, who was also believed to be dead, and the former partners made a deal: Stromm would use his knowledge of robotics technology to create weapons for Osborn's far-reaching revenge scheme against Spider-Man, and Osborn would one day employ the services of one of his agents, geneticist Seward Trainer, to restore Stromm's body to youth and vitality.

ALAS... I CANNOT!

BUT I WILL TAKE THE SMALL VICTORIES -- SUCH AS THIS -- WHERE I FIND THEM!

Stromm, now outfitted in an armored life-support suit and calling himself Gaunt, conducted a campaign of terrorism and intimidation against Peter Parker and Ben Reilly, who was wearing the Spider-Man costume at the time. These attempts at throwing them off the trail were unsuccessful, however, and Spider-Man and the then-powerless Parker stopped Gaunt's personal scheme to restore his body with Trainer's aid. Later, however, Trainer repeated the experiment success-fully, and Stromm, once again hale and hearty, was outfitted in a new exoskeleton that made him a virtual walking arsenal. He still met defeat at Spidey's hands, however, and is currently in custody.

LOOTER

Eccentric would-be scientist Norton G. Fester began his super-criminal career with the discovery of a mysterious meteor that he was convinced held the secrets of the universe! Unable to receive funding for his oddball, unsubstantiated theories, Fester studied the meteor himself, and was exposed to a blast of strange gas from within it. He soon realized that, amazingly, the gas had endowed him with superhuman strength and stamina. Now more concerned with the accumulation of wealth for its own sake rather than further scientific studies, Fester donned a garish costume, called himself the Looter, and used his newfound, meteor-borne abilities to conduct a one-man crime wave.

Inevitably, the Looter ran afoul of Spider-Man, who managed to defeat Fester and send him to prison. Fester escaped on several subsequent occasions, only to continually fall in defeat to the web-slinger.

Fester's most recent criminal exploits were in the employ of the new Doctor Octopus, where he used cybernetic enhancements to augment his own natural strength, and thereafter as an independent thief, purloining a veritable arsenal of super-weaponry from other villains. Once again, he was accumulating wealth—but oddly enough, this time for the purpose of funding his study of yet another meteor... which he still delusionally believes holds the key to the mysteries of the universe!

SILVERMANE

Silvio Manfredi was barely a lad off the boat from the old country when he got involved with organized crime in America. Nicknamed "Silvermane" for his prematurely white mane of hair, he rose quickly to the head of his "family" and over the course of his long career, formed a formidable international drug trafficking organization.

Learning of the existence of an ancient stone tablet that reputedly could restore youth, Silvermane set out to steal it for himself, and had his first encounter with Spider-Man. Spidey rescued the hostages Silver-mane had taken in the course of his scheme, but was unable to prevent the aged crimelord from using the tablet to restore his youth.

Silvermane's criminal career branched out afterward into an alliance with the subversive organization HYDRA and a gangwar with the third Green Goblin. Silvermane was grievously injured in this final conflict, the shock of which undid the effects of the rejuvenation process, rendering him once again old and feeble and in need of special life-support machinery to stay alive. Silvermane's cunning mind and brilliant strategical skills, however, remain unaffected and, despite his infirmities, Silvermane continues to be a major player in East Coast organized crime and a thorn in the wall-crawler's side.

MORBIUS

Driven by a thirst for human blood, Michael Morbius has been cursed to lead a life of mind-numbing horror. For years he's sought to free himself from his ghoulish compulsion, but he's met with only infrequent and temporary success.

Although not a true vampire, Morbius acquired the characteristics of one when he applied his skills as a Nobel Prize-winning biochemist to concoct a serum to cure himself of a rare blood disease. The serum eventually saved him, but at a terrible cost—he now required the blood of others to replace his own degenerating blood. He also gained super-strength, fangs and an ashen pallor. Over the years, his savage bloodlust has led to many brutal encounters with Spider-Man.

Recently, Morbius has lost control over his needs, and has started attacking innocent people to satisfy his thirst. He still maintains an unhealthy interest in Spider-Man, as he is convinced that the wall-crawler's irradiated blood holds the cure for his own nightmarish condition.

SPIDER-SLAYERS

--IT'S TIME FOR ALISTAIR SMYTHE TO TAKE HIS ALL NEW CYBERSLAYERS ON A LITTLE FIELD TEST!

Designed for the sole purpose of killing Spider-Man, the Spider-Slayers are as terrifying a group of attackers as the wall-crawler has ever faced. First designed by Spencer Smythe and underwritten by J. Jonah Jameson, the Spider-Slayer robots were redesigned and improved after each failed encounter with the web-slinger—but ultimately to no avail. In the end, Spencer Smythe died unfulfilled, his body poisoned by the very radioactive elements which he used to power his robot assassins.

In a determined attempt to end the family tradition of failure, Spencer's son Alistair Smythe directed a group of mechanical experts in building new Spider-Slayers. Smythe also had his own body cybernetically re-engineered, becoming the self-styled Ultimate Spider-Slayer! Super-strong and equipped with wall-crawling and web-spinning abilities similar to Spidey's, Smythe's robot army seemed unbeatable. But Spider-Man defeated them anyway and shut down Smythe's Spider-Slayer factory as well.

Smythe continues to plot his revenge on Spidey, constantly improving his killing machines in the fervent hope that one day they'll be able to finish the job his father began years earlier.

SPIDER-MAN RATES HIS OPPONENTS

*Thanks to my spider-powers,
normal criminals don't pose much of a threat to me.
But there are some "normal" bad guys who have
made themselves so skillful in one method of fighting
or another that they can even give a guy with the
proportionate strength of a spider a hard time!*

HAMMERHEAD (sans exo-skeleton)
KINGPIN
PUNISHER
ROSE

*Then there are criminals who can't match me in strength,
but make up for it with unusual weapons and gimmickry!*

BEETLE
SHOCKER

*Other menaces who can't match my strength have other
kinds of super-powers that make them real threats to me!*

ELECTRO
HYDRO-MAN
MORBIUS

*A lot of my longtime enemies are roughly as strong as
I am, and over the years many of them have grown in
fighting skill just as I have! You never know how my fights
with these guys will go, 'cause we're so evenly matched!*

DOCTOR OCTOPUS
DOCTOR OCTOPUS II
GAUNT
KRAVEN THE HUNTER
LIZARD
LOOTER
TOMBSTONE
HAMMERHEAD (with exo-skeleton)
TENDRIL
VERMIN

Some of my sparring partners have just a slight edge on me strength-wise. Combined with their other abilities, this makes them particularly dangerous!

KAINE
PUMA
SCORPION
WILL O'THE WISP

I really have to watch my step with enemies who are roughly twice as strong as I am, like these guys.

MOLTEN MAN
VENOM

But then I've had opponents who are five times stronger than I am, or even more! It takes a combination of my greater agility and my years of combat experience to cope with their brute strength!

CARNAGE
RHINO
SANDMAN

My worst enemies aren't necessarily the ones who are the best in hand-to-hand fighting. They're the ones who manipulate their pawns—and me—from behind the scenes! They can turn my whole life upside down before I even know they're back in business!

CHAMELEON
GREEN GOBLIN I
GREEN GOBLIN II
HOBGOBLIN I
JACKAL
MYSTERIO

BEN REILLY

For half a decade Ben Reilly wandered the United States, believing he had no true identity to call his own. Then, for a brief time, he believed he had a role in the world as the heroic Spider-Man, before his very life was taken from him.

Ben Reilly was a clone created from Spider-Man's DNA years ago by the demented genetic engineer Miles Warren, alias the Jackal, to combat the real Spider-Man. He had all of Peter Parker's memories, but believed himself to be no more than a copy of a real man. In despair, the clone left New York City to begin an aimless existence, moving from one city and job to another for the next five years. He named himself Ben Reilly, after Peter Parker's deceased uncle and Peter's Aunt May's maiden name.

Finally returning to New York to visit the dying Aunt May, Ben encountered the real Peter Parker. They became not only allies but virtually saw themselves as brothers. For a time, Ben returned to crimefighting in a new costumed identity, the Scarlet Spider.

But then, Ben and Peter performed tests that seemed to indicate that it was Peter who was the clone, not Ben. Peter and Ben came to an agreement: Peter gave up his life as a crimefighter and moved to Portland, Oregon with his pregnant wife Mary Jane, to raise their baby in peace, while Ben stayed in New York and eventually assumed the role of Spider-Man.

ALLIES

MUCH DIFFERENT...

Neither Ben nor Peter realized that they were pawns being manipulated by one of Spider-Man's greatest enemies, Norman Osborn, the original Green Goblin. Osborn sought to revenge himself on his nemesis by causing him to disbelieve in his own identity. Finally, in open combat the Green Goblin murdered the new Spider-Man, and Ben's clone body melted back into basic protoplasm. Now knowing the truth, the mournful Peter Parker resumed his career as Spider-Man.

Though Ben Reilly had but a brief existence of six years, he was far from a mere copy of a real man. In both his life as Spider-Man and his heroic death he proved himself as great a hero as the original.

BLACK CAT

Felicia Hardy could be said to be a second generation criminal. Upon learning that her father had once been a notorious cat burglar, she decided to follow in his footsteps. To her, the dangers of a life of crime would fill her formerly humdrum existence with excitement. Updating her father's modus operandi for an age of super heroes, Felicia donned a costume and became the Black Cat.

Although she had no actual super powers, the Black Cat was an extraordinary athlete. Beyond that, she staged "accidents" designed to convince her adversaries that, as a "black cat," she had the power to give those who crossed her path bad luck.

The one who crossed her path the most often was Spider-Man, on whom she quickly developed a crush. Ultimately she was caught, unmasked, and sent to prison, but she feigned insanity and escaped. Then, still enamored with Spider-Man, she began fighting criminals alongside him and soon won a pardon for her past crimes.

By now, Spider-Man had fallen in love with her, dazzled by a woman who could share his life of adventure. But when he revealed his true identity to her, the deeply immature Cat was disappointed that he was merely an "ordinary" guy beneath his mask. After she was seriously injured in combat with Doctor Octopus, Spider-Man decided to end their partnership, saying it was too dangerous for her.

Desperate to gain super-powers, Felicia made a deal with an anonymous man to perform services for him in exchange for his giving her the powers she sought. His scientists did indeed give her heightened, catlike agility and the actual power to cause people bad luck. But then Felicia learned that her benefactor was one of Spider-Man's greatest foes, the Kingpin.

Learning of Felicia's connection with the Kingpin, Spider-Man broke off their relationship as partners and lovers. Afterwards, Felicia tried to antagonize her ex-boyfriend by dallying for a time with his adversary, the Foreigner. Later, she returned to New York and began dating Flash Thompson in her civilian identity to make Peter jealous. But she actually fell in love with Flash, and was devastated when he finally broke up with her.

Today the Black Cat no longer has her bad luck powers, but she has completely reformed. She and Spider-Man are now friends, and she operates her own private security agency, Cat's Eye.

ALLIES

DAREDEVIL

Early in his career, Spider-Man saved a seemingly helpless blind man from a gang of muggers. Little did he suspect that this man, lawyer Matt Murdock, would prove to be one of his most staunch allies—Daredevil, the Man without Fear! Daredevil's other senses are superhumanly acute, and he possesses a radar sense that more than compensates for his inability to see.

Soon afterwards, Spider-Man went to investigate a performance by a circus whose posters advertised him as a special guest star—without bothering to ask him! The head of the circus proved to be the Ringmaster of Crime, who used the hypnotic device concealed in his top hat to mesmerize both Spider-Man and the audience. Luckily, Matt Murdock was also in attendance, and his blindness ironically safeguarded him against the Ringmaster's hypnosis. He charged into action in his costumed identity of Daredevil, but the Ringmaster ordered Spider-Man to stop him. Daredevil's own extraordinary acrobatic skills enabled him to hold his own against the far stronger Spider-Man until he could seize the Ringmaster's hat and use it to bring the web-slinger out of his trance.

Since then Daredevil and Spider-Man have teamed up repeatedly over the years against adversaries ranging from the Masked Marauder to the demon Blackheart. Most recently, they teamed up against the conclave of organized crime bosses convened by Fortunato.

Daredevil's superhuman hearing enabled him to discover that Peter Parker and Spider-Man had the same heartbeat pattern and hence were the same person. In turn, Spider-Man eventually learned Daredevil's true identity as well. Their knowledge of each other's closely guarded secrets has proved to be a bond further uniting these two crimefighters as allies.

ALLIES

HUMAN TORCH

Spider-Man is a loner, perennially misunderstood and held in suspicion by much of the public. The Human Torch, on the other hand, is a member of the first modern super hero team, the Fantastic Four, and is acclaimed worldwide as a hero. But it is what the Torch and Spider-Man have in common that made them friends. When they first met, they were both teenagers, endowed with super powers by accident and thrust into lives of danger and adventure.

Johnny Storm accompanied his sister Susan, her fiancee Dr. Reed Richards, and their friend Ben Grimm on a fateful unauthorized test flight of the starship Richards had built for the U.S. government. An unexpected cosmic storm bombarded the craft with radiation, mutating the passengers. Johnny gained the power to generate flame from his body without harm to himself, and called himself the Human Torch, after the legendary super hero of World War II.

Spider-Man first met the Torch when he invaded the Fantastic Four's headquarters in an unsuccessful bid to persuade them to hire him as a fifth member of the team. Soon afterwards, though, all of Spider-Man's confidence was knocked out of him when he first fought Doctor Octopus and was beaten for the very first time. A despairing Peter Parker then attended a speech given by Johnny Storm. When Johnny advised the audience never to give up, no matter what their troubles, Peter was inspired to go back and defeat his foe.

Eventually, Spider-Man and the Torch found themselves teaming up against foes like the Green Goblin, the Fox, the Sandman, the Enforcers, and the Beetle. They even established a regular meeting place atop the Statue of Liberty.

Spider-Man has not trusted the Torch with his secret identity, and, though Johnny knows Peter Parker, he regards him as something of an annoyance. Spider-Man and the Torch continually trade bantering insults, in a mix of humor and a kind of sibling rivalry. But underneath it all is a genuine respect for one another, and each would risk his life to save the other.

MOLTEN MAN

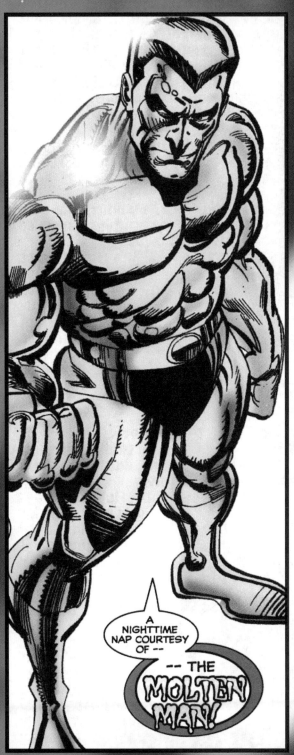

A NIGHTTIME NAP COURTESY OF --

-- THE MOLTEN MAN!

Like the Sandman, the Molten Man offers proof that even one of Spider-Man's most lethal opponents can have the potential to change for the better. In the case of the Molten Man, he became not only Spider-Man's ally but his friend.

The half-brother of Peter Parker's high school classmate Liz Allan, Mark Raxton was the assistant to Spencer Smythe, the creator of the original Spider-Slayer robots. Together they developed a strange liquid metal alloy. Thinking it would make him a fortune, the greedy Raxton struck Smythe down and seized a sample of the alloy. But in the melee, the liquid metal spilled over him, sheathing his entire body with a golden, metallic coating which somehow endowed Raxton with superhuman strength. Reveling in his new power, Raxton turned to crime, only to be stopped time and again by Spider-Man.

Eventually the metal alloy melded with Raxton's skin, further increasing his strength and inducing a strange chemical reaction that caused his body to radiate intense heat.

In time, the reaction came to an end, but the Molten Man retained his golden, rock-hard skin and his great strength. But over the years Raxton matured and reformed. He was reconciled with his half-sister Liz, and he and his former enemy Spider-Man have since joined forces to oppose the schemes of her husband, Harry Osborn, the second Green Goblin.

ALLIES

PROWLER

Hobie Brown wanted to win fame and fortune as an inventor, but instead he found himself trapped in a menial job as a window washer. Then he came up with what he thought was a brilliant plan. He created a costume incorporating his inventions, named himself the Prowler, and stole the Daily Bugle payroll. He intended to return the money as Hobie Brown, claiming he had recovered it from the Prowler, and be acclaimed as a hero. As the Prowler, Hobie wore steel-tipped gauntlets that enabled him to scale walls. His principal weapons were bracelets that could fire pellets containing gases, explosives, or magnesium flares.

But Hobie's plan ran into a considerable obstacle: Spider-Man. Although the Prowler initially managed to hold Spider-Man off, when they next met Spider-Man easily overpowered and unmasked him. But when Spider-Man learned Hobie's story, he let Hobie go.

Hobie eventually found employment as a construction worker, and then finally found work in electronics engineering. By then he had finally married his longtime girlfriend Mindy McPherson.

But from time to time over the years, Hobie has briefly resumed his Prowler guise, fascinated by the idea of becoming a costumed crimefighter. The Prowler worked briefly as an operative for Silver Sable in the team known as the Outlaws. Later, he successfully overcame the Vulture on his own.

But Hobie always ends up by putting his costume aside until the temptation of his other identity once again becomes too strong to resist. Most recently, he tried to earn money as the Prowler by participating in the "Great Game" of combats between costumed opponents sponsored by millionaires, only to end up seriously injured. Only time will tell if Hobie Brown will ever become the Prowler again.

ALLIES

EMPIRE STATE UNIVERSITY

Upon graduating from Midtown High, Peter Parker entered Empire State University in Manhattan's Greenwich Village, where he majored in biology. It was here that late bloomer Peter emerged from his shell. He forged close, lasting friendships with many of his fellow students, including his former nemesis, Flash Thompson; Harry Osborn, who became his roommate; and Peter's future wife Mary Jane Watson. And it was in college that Peter fell deeply in love with his classmate Gwen Stacy, only to suffer through her murder by Harry's father, the Green Goblin.

After graduating college, Peter stayed on at ESU as a graduate student. During his first graduate stint, he worked for Dr. Morris Sloan as a teaching assistant and dated Sloan's secretary, Debra Whitman. After leaving ESU for a time, he resumed his studies there and became a lab assistant for Dr. Evan Swann.

A surprising number of Spider-Man's enemies were connected with ESU, including the Foolkiller, the Lightmaster, and the deadliest of all, Professor Miles Warren, aka the Jackal.

Peter has recently returned to his studies at ESU once more. It remains to be seen if he will ever get his Ph.D.

GWEN STACY
Peter's girlfriend and classmate

HARRY OSBORN
Peter's classmate and roommate

MARY JANE WATSON
Peter's girlfriend and classmate

EUGENE "FLASH" THOMPSON
Classmate

"-- BUT HERE, TOO, AT MY ALMA MATER, MIDTOWN HIGH SCHOOL!

"(AND WHY THEY NAMED A HIGH SCHOOL IN QUEENS 'MIDTOWN', WHEN MIDTOWN'S ACROSS THE RIVER IN MANHATTAN; I'LL NEVER KNOW!)

"THIS IS WHERE I SPEND MY TIME, FIVE DAYS A WEEK, WHEN I'M NOT COMING UP WITH EXCUSES TO DUCK OUT AND FIGHT SUPER-VILLAINS --

MIDTOWN HIGH SCHOOL

MIDTOWN HIGH SCHOOL

The teenage Peter Parker was only a sophomore at Midtown High, his neighborhood high school, when he attended the fateful demonstration during which he acquired his superhuman powers.

Peter had no close friends at Midtown High. He was bullied and insulted, however, by the school's football star, Flash Thompson. Flash's clique, including Liz Allan, Sally Avril, Jason Ionello, and Tiny McKeever, shunned the studious Peter.

Despite his unhappy time there, the adult Peter once returned for a Midtown High class reunion. Still later, Peter served as a substitute teacher at Midtown High. He was shocked to discover that, within less than a decade, the neighborhood and the school had gone sharply downhill, from a conservative middle-class milieu to a potentially dangerous inner city environment.

DAILY  BUGLE

NEW YORK'S FINEST DAILY NEWSPAPER

The Daily Bugle, a prominent New York City newspaper published in midtown Manhattan, has been both Peter Parker's friend and enemy. Its publisher J. Jonah Jameson has delivered scathing editorial attacks on Spider-Man from the beginning of his crimefighting career. Yet Jameson has also employed Peter Parker as a freelance photographer since his high school years. Ironically, Peter's chief value to the Bugle has been to supply photographs of himself as Spider-Man in battle (thanks to an automatic camera), which Jameson then uses to illustrate his anti-Spider-Man tirades.

There have been only two interruptions in Peter's association with Jameson and the Bugle. For a brief time, Peter switched to doing photography for one of the Bugle's competitors, the Daily Globe. Later, Thomas Fireheart (alias the Puma) temporarily took control of the Bugle, but finally sold it back to Jameson.

Peter has made many friends on the Bugle staff, notably editor in chief Joe "Robbie" Robertson, who takes a paternal interest in him, and reporter Betty Brant, whom Peter dated when she was Jameson's secretary. Other friends on staff include reporter Ben Urich and Jameson's current secretary Glory Grant.

Over the years several Bugle employees Peter knew have died, including reporters Frederick Foswell (who was once the criminal mastermind, the Big Man) and Ned Leeds (who was mistaken for the Hobgoblin) and photographers Nick Katzenberg and Lance Bannon.

Recently Peter was finally hired as a Bugle staff photographer. But thanks to the renowned Parker luck, he was almost immediately laid off, along with reporter Jake Conover and city editor Kate Cushing.

◀ **J. JONAH JAMESON**
Publisher

JOE ROBERTSON ▶
Editor in Chief

◀ **BETTY BRANT**
Reporter

BEN URICH ▶
Reporter

◀ **GLORIA "GLORY"
GRANT**
Jameson's Secretary

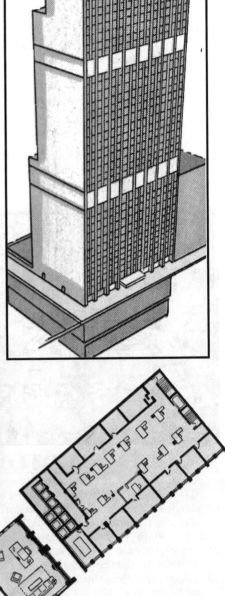

WILL O'THE WISP

The eeriest of Spider-Man's allies is a being whose ghostlike appearance and powers make him seem the embodiment of his name, the Will o'the Wisp.

Jackson Arvad was a scientist employed by the Brand Corporation, an unscrupulous scientific research and development firm. In a terrible accident, Arvad fell into a magno-chamber whose electromagnetic field weakened the bonds between the molecules of his body, causing them to begin to disperse. His ruthless employer, James Melvin, after cross-examining Arvad about what had happened, left him trapped in the magno-chamber to die.

But Arvad discovered that he had gained new superhuman abilities and escaped from Brand. From then onward, he could alter the density of his body. He could now become so light that he could fly, or even attain intangibility. Alternatively, he could will himself to become as hard as rock, with superhuman strength. He had become the being known as Will o'the Wisp.

However, each time after he reduced his body's density, he found it more difficult to resume solid form. Desperate, Arvad sought out the criminal scientist Dr. Jonas Harrow for help. The treacherous Harrow implanted a device in Arvad's skull that could disrupt his control over his powers. Harrow then forced Arvad to commit crimes on his behalf.

This led to the Will o'the Wisp's first clash with Spider-Man, who tried to persuade him to turn against Harrow. Finally, Arvad rebelled, only to be dissipated by Harrow into seeming oblivion.

But that was not the end. The Will o'the Wisp's consciousness was still intact, and he found a means to force scientist Dr. Marla Madison to restore him to solid form. He then sought to kill Melvin, whom he blamed for his plight, but finally chose instead to cooperate with Spider-Man in bringing Melvin and Brand to justice.

On occasion the Will o'the Wisp has allied himself with Spider-Man, and was once a member of the Outlaws, one of Silver Sable's teams of superhuman mercenaries. But since his transformation, Arvad's personality has radically changed. He is not only vengeful but often seems eerily inhuman. He has fought Spider-Man almost as often as he has aided him, and it seems that two such radically different personalities could never truly be friends.

SILVER SABLE

Spider-Man has had one of the longest careers of any modern super hero. But to one of his sometime allies, he is still an untrained newcomer.

That person is the world's most famous mercenary leader, Silver Sable.

Born in the tiny nation of Symkaria in Europe's Balkan Mountains, Silver Sable was the daughter of Ernst Sablinovia, the leader of the Wild Pack, a team of highly trained combatants dedicated to tracking down Nazi war criminals. After Ernst disappeared, Silver took over the leadership of the Wild Pack. Today, Silver Sable and her Wild Pack primarily operate as the world's leading teams of mercenaries, although they only accept missions of which Silver morally approves. The large fees they earn from their clients throughout the world are a major source of income for Symkaria.

Silver Sable herself is a master strategist and a highly formidable hand-to-hand combatant. Besides her mercenary activities, she is also a leading figure in international society, a leading representative of Symkaria, and even a renowned fashion model.

On many occasions when Silver Sable's operations have brought her to New York City, Spider-Man has worked with her, sometimes as a paid freelance agent. Spider-Man even journeyed to Symkaria once to help Sable combat "The Assassin Nation Plot," in which the Red Skull brought about the assassination of the nation's prime minister.

A consummate professional, Silver Sable initially regarded Spider-Man as a mere amateur in her business of hunting down criminals. But as time has passed, she has developed a grudging respect for him.

Ironically, she employs his old enemy, the Sandman, as one of her prioncipal agents, and was once married to another of his foes, the Foreigner. She also once led the Outlaws, a team that comprised many of Spider-Man's past allies and adversaries, including the Prowler, the Rocket Racer, the Sandman, and Will o' the Wisp.

NOT AT ALL!

SANDMAN

Of the ten allies of Spider-Man profiled here, the one with the strangest abilities was also once one of his deadliest and most formidable enemies. Over all the years that the Sandman tried to kill Spider-Man, neither of them ever dreamed they would one day fight side-by-side.

William Baker's father abandoned him and his mother when William was only three years old, reducing them to poverty. As he grew up, William drifted into crime, eventually becoming notorious under the alias Flint Marko.

After escaping from prison, Marko hid out on a beach near a military testing site. When a reactor there exploded, Marko was bombarded with radiation that mutated him, enabling him to transform his body into a form that mimicked the properties of the sand around him. He could now assume any shape he wished, will himself to become as hard as granite—with superhuman strength to match—or disperse his body into scattered grains and then reassemble himself.

Marko was far more dangerous than before, but time and again his one-man crime waves were thwarted by Spider-Man. The Sandman joined the Sinister Six in an effort to crush his foe, and later became a founding member of the Fantastic Four's criminal counterparts, the Frightful Four.

Finally, Sandman teamed with Hydro-Man, a criminal who could similarly turn his body into water, in a new effort to defeat Spider-Man. In the course of the battle, Sandman and Hydro-Man were accidentally merged into a single, mud-like creature. When Sandman finally regained his separate identity, he was so shaken by the experience that he decided to reform.

For a time, Sandman worked with the Avengers as a trainee, but is now in the employ of the mercenary leader Silver Sable. He has aided Spider-Man on missions with Sable, and has even joined forces with Spider-Man against the rest of the Sinister Six.

PUNISHER

In most of Spider-Man's battles, the division between his friends and his enemies is clear. Sometimes, as with the Molten Man and Sandman, an enemy can cross the line and become an ally. Likewise, a friend like Harry Osborn can become an implacable enemy. But one man straddles the line between ally and adversary: the Punisher.

A veteran soldier and former student for the priesthood, Frank Castle was picnicking in Manhattan's Central Park with his wife and young children when they inadvertently witnessed a gangland execution. The mobsters gunned down the Castle family, leaving them for dead. But Frank Castle survived, and in time reemerged as the Punisher, a costumed vigilante obsessed with meting out death to all criminals who had somehow escaped the reach of the law.

Early in the Punisher's one-man war against crime, he formed an alliance with the Jackal, mistakenly thinking they shared similar goals.

The Jackal persuaded the Punisher that Spider-Man was yet another criminal deserving of his brand of justice. Thus Spider-Man and the Punisher first met as enemies, but the web-slinger soon convinced Castle that the Jackal, not he, was the real criminal.

Since then, Spider-Man and the Punisher have crossed paths repeatedly, taking on such opponents as Jigsaw, the Tarantula, Dr. Octopus and the Secret Empire. But theirs is an uneasy alliance. The Punisher believes Spider-Man's refusal to take a life is a sign of weakness. Spider-Man is haunted by guilt over his failure to bring the Punisher to justice, thereby allowing him to continue his killings. Ultimately, though, the Punisher and Spider-Man recognize that they have the same goal—to safeguard the innocent—and so they cooperate when it serves their mutual purpose.

Spider-Man made his debut in AMAZING FANTASY #15, cover-dated August 1962, in a story scripted by Stan Lee and illustrated by Steve Ditko. In this, the final issue of one of Marvel's science fiction anthology comics of the early 1960s, Stan decided to experiment with creating a super hero unlike any other ever before seen. Despite his super-powers, Peter Parker would be portrayed as a realistic teenager, experiencing emotions and personal problems that anyone growing up could identify with. Moreover, Lee and Ditko intended to show what Peter's life as Spider-Man would be like in a world recognizably like our own, in which good did not always triumph and even a hero could be mistrusted and feared by the people he sought to help.

This first story in AMAZING FANTASY #15 presented Spider-Man's entire origin, from the radioactive spider biting the bookworm Peter Parker through Spider-Man's brief, self-centered show business career to the shocking death of his Uncle Ben. It introduced Peter's Aunt May and Uncle Ben and his schoolmates Flash Thompson and Liz Allan. The climax comes when Spider-Man captures the killer, only to realize that he was the same burglar Spidey had refused to stop earlier at the television studio. The story concludes with the lesson Spider-Man learned from this tragedy, words which motivated his entire crimefighting career: "With great power, there must also come great responsibility."